978 0741612366

This book
is dedicated to:

_____

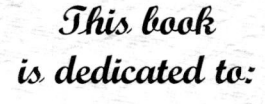

From

_____

© 2002 Havoc Publishing
San Diego, California
U.S.A.

Text by F.E. Skarka

ISBN 0-7416-1236-4

All rights reserved.
No part of this publication may be reproduced or transmitted in any form or by any means, electronic or mechanical, including photocopying, recording, any information storage and retrieval system without permission in writing from the publisher.

www.havocpub.com

Made in China

Footprints

"...During your times of trial and suffering, when you saw only one set of footprints, it was then that the Lord carried you."

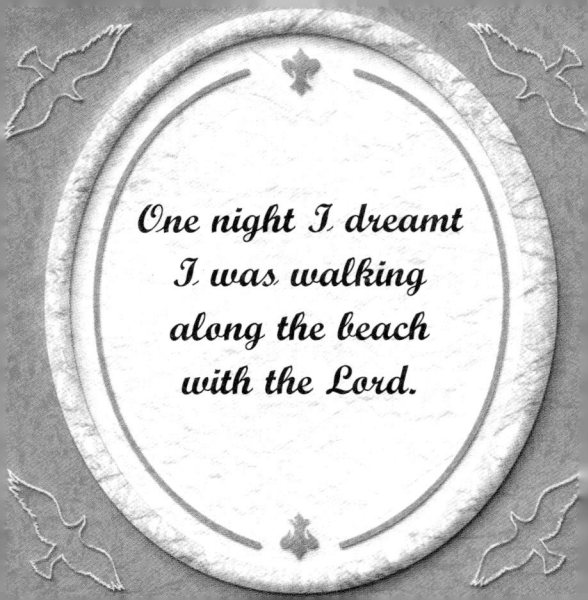

Many scenes from my life flashed across the sky. In each scene I noticed footprints in the sand.

So I said to the Lord,
"You promised me, Lord,
that if I followed you,
you would
walk with me always."

The Lord replied,
"The times when
you have seen
only one set of footprints
is when I carried you."

*When the skies
turn dark with clouds
and winds begin to blow,
the Lord leads
His children
to the safety
of their homes.*

When the clouds disappear and light pours from the heavens, the Lord leads His children to play in the warmth of His light.

*The Lord's light
is always there
to show you the way.*

*If ever your legs should tire
or your back fails to bend,
the Lord will lift
and carry you
until you are strong again.*

*The Lord's children
will be safe
in the darkest of nights
when they trust to follow
the love of His light.*

The Lord's children
need not be afraid;
the Lord is
always with them.

*With His light
to lead you,
you shall
find your way.*

The Lord's children
know He is near
and His love
will keep them strong
as they continue
on their journeys
to the beauty
of His song.

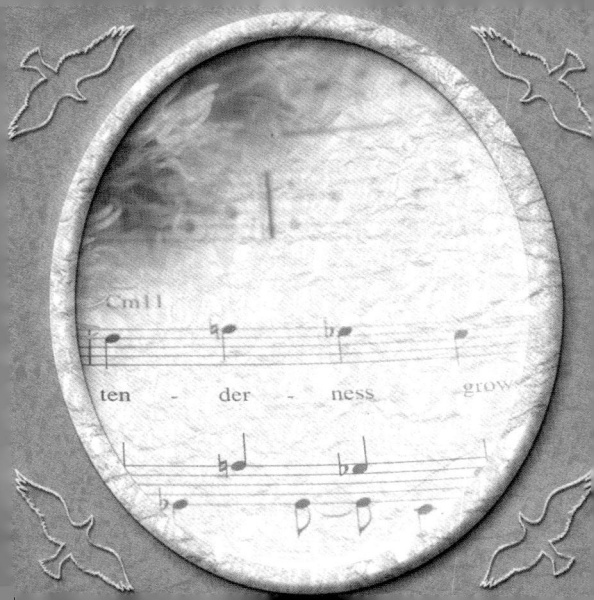

*No matter how heavy
His children,
the Lord
carries them home.*

The Lord is
beside His children
and there He will
forever stay.

Days when clouds covered the sun and days when rain slowly poured,

*The Lord's children
need not worry.
The Lord will
care for them.*

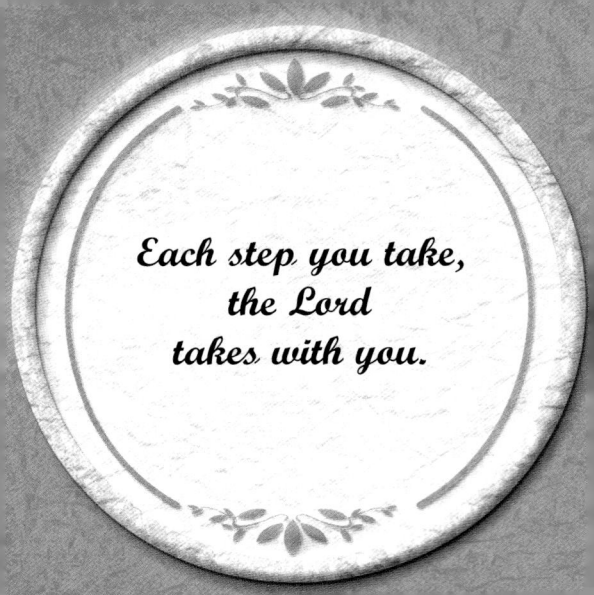

The Lord is with you during the hardest of times and the best of times.

You will never
call for the Lord
as He is
always beside you.

When clouds cover the sun
and all light slides away,
the Lord is a friend
to help His children
on their way.

And when light pours
from the sky
and the day
is bright and new,
the Lord is still
beside His children
in everything they do.

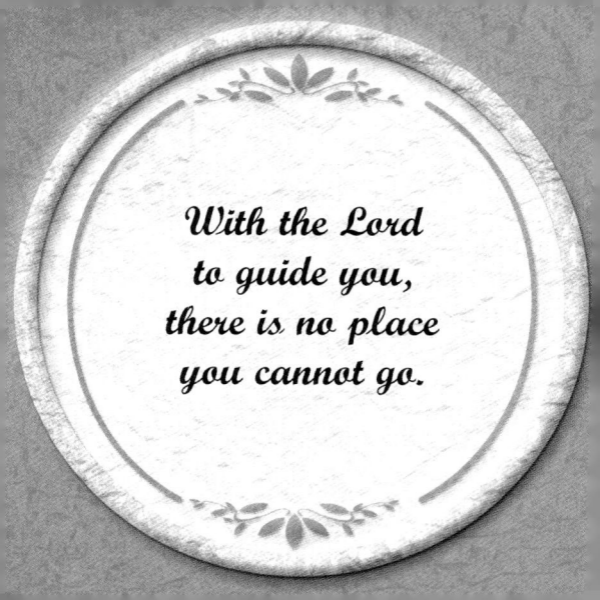

With the Lord to guide you, there is no place you cannot go.

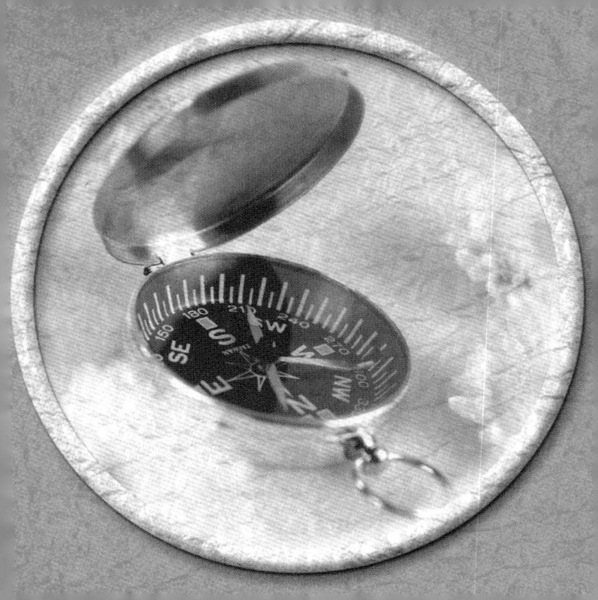
150
180
210
240
270
SE
S
W
NW
E

*When your journey
is finished
you will find
the Lord has been with you
all the way.*

*You are never lost
as your journey
is the Lord's.*

The Lord is
the shepherd
who counts
His sheep
before the night
turns black,

and all the lost
will be found
for He will
bring them back.

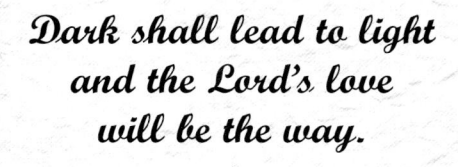

Dark shall lead to light and the Lord's love will be the way.

*You stand in
the Lord's light,
so warm in His love.*

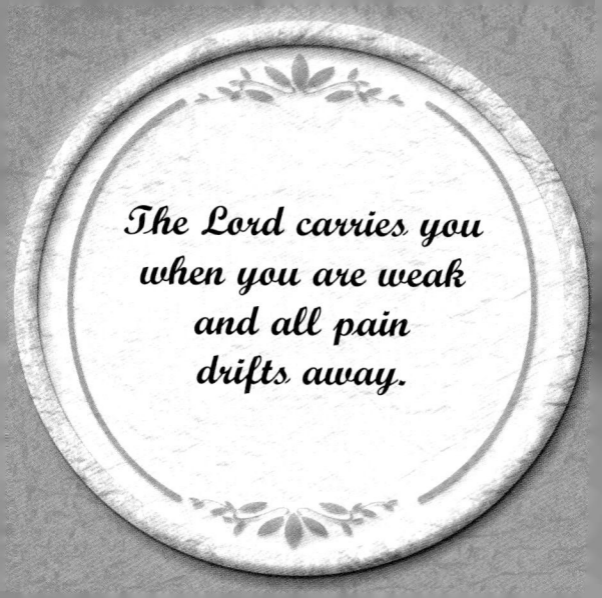

The Lord carries you
when you are weak
and all pain
drifts away.

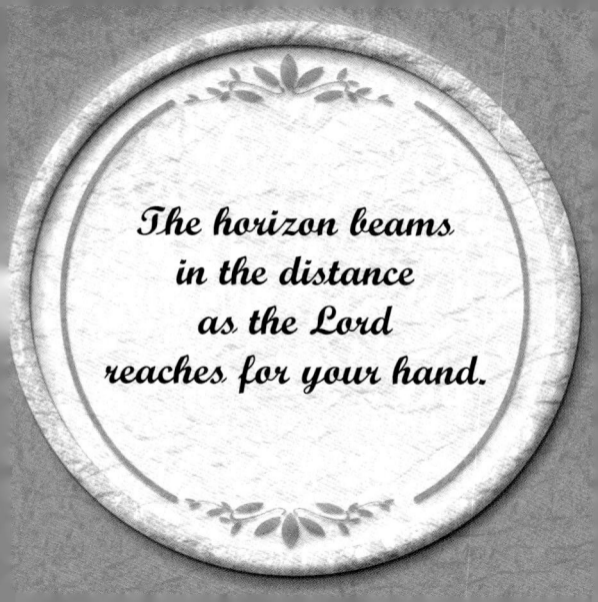

The horizon beams
in the distance
as the Lord
reaches for your hand.

You are never lost
for the Lord is
close by your side.
You shall never fear
for He is your guide.

The Lord's children will find the Lord on the path of their journeys.

*All the way
they will know
the wonder
of His light.*

The Lord is everywhere
and all at once:
blowing clouds
through the sky,
opening flowers to bloom,
lifting birds in flight.

His love is everywhere:
running beside children
in June,
singing babies into sleep,
with the softness
of His song.

The Lord is with you
all the time,
in times of despair
and joy.

The Lord's children
are safe in His care,
as He shelters them
with love.

*When you were searching,
you found Him.
When you were weak,
He was there.*

The times when
you are most in need
He comforts you
with care.

The Lord's love is a candle that burns forever bright.

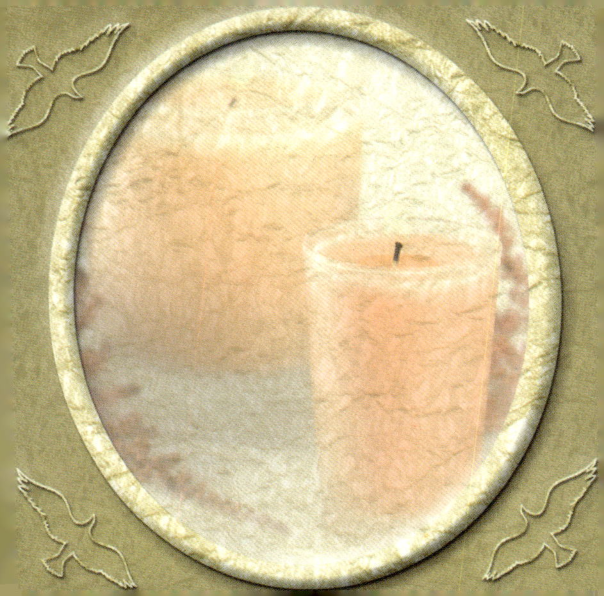

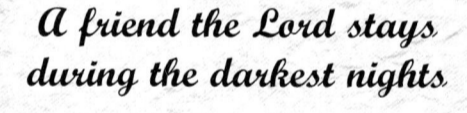

A friend the Lord stays during the darkest nights

and the hardest days, guiding with careful love.

The Lord gently carries His children in the safety of His arms.

The night
turned dark
and He was there,
casting light
to guide the way.

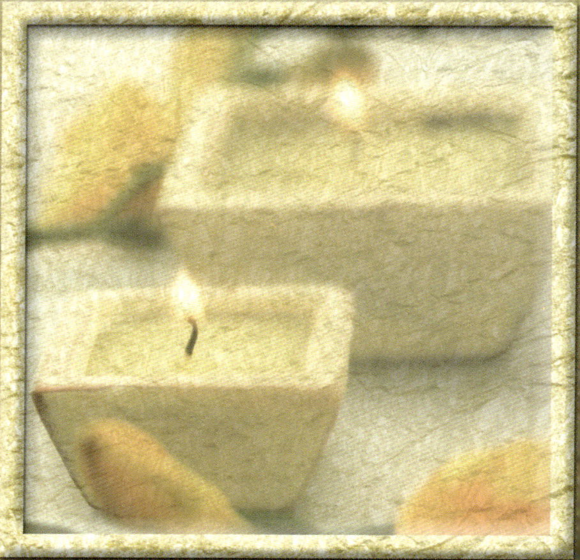

The day
is so much brighter
when lit by the Lord.

When you want
the Lord
He calls for you
and keeps you safe
from harm.

*The Lord is
beside His children
like the shepherd
beside His sheep.*

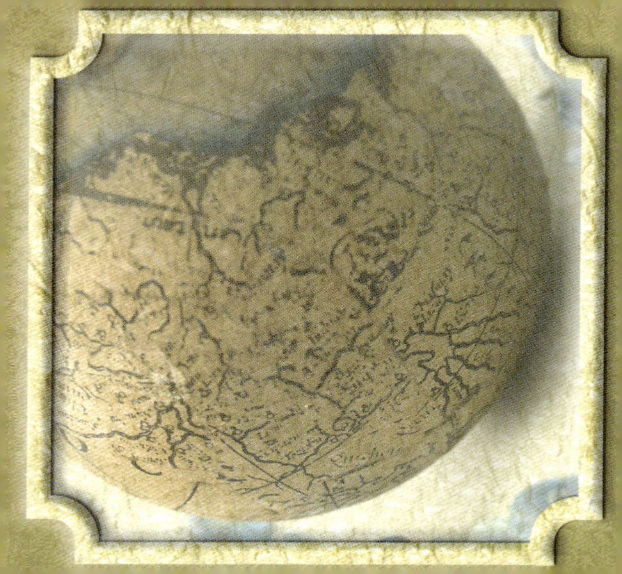

*The Lord is
with His children always,
wherever they should
travel.*

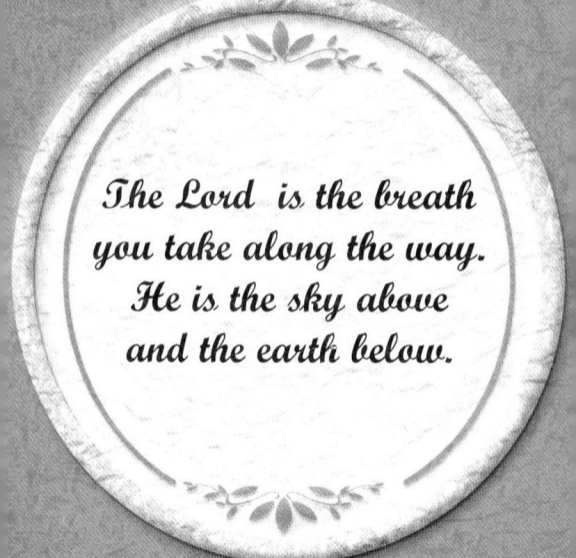

The Lord is the breath
you take along the way.
He is the sky above
and the earth below.

*He is the wind
that brings ships
to their homes,
safely to the shore.*

The road turned away
toward the dark
and the Lord's hand
stretched out to you.
The road rose
over the mountain
and His strength
helped you climb.

Your journey is filled
with many turns
but His guidance has
helped you through.
His guidance is
with you all the time
to share the
wonders of your life.

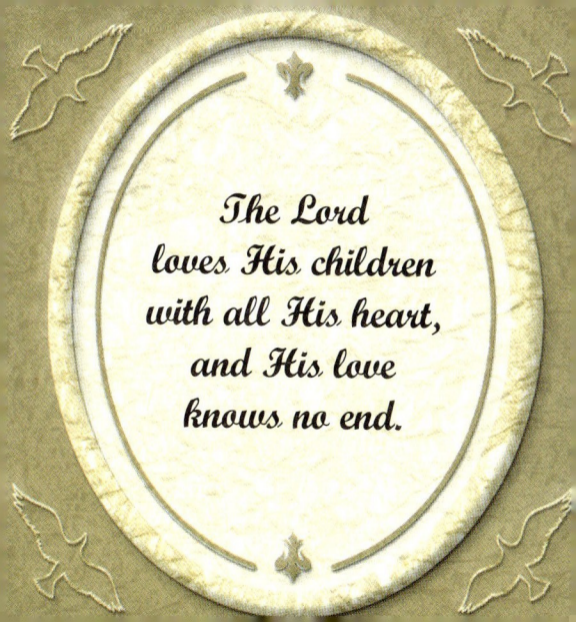

The Lord
loves His children
with all His heart,
and His love
knows no end.

Your journey you share with the Lord, and His love will be yours forever.

You are never
cold or hungry
as the Lord
is always with you.

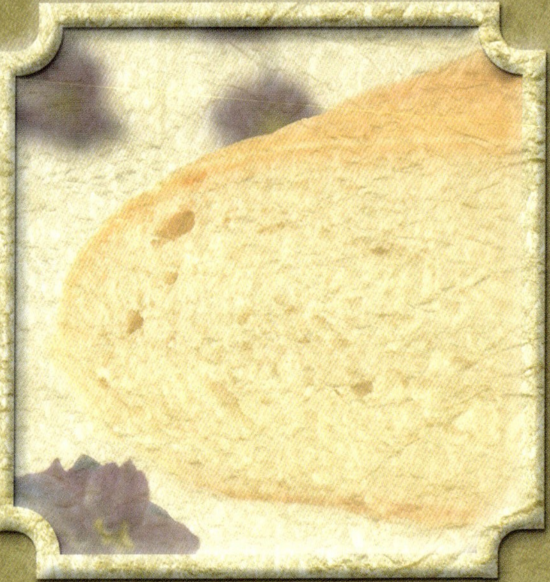

The Lord's love
is the light that leads
the way towards home.

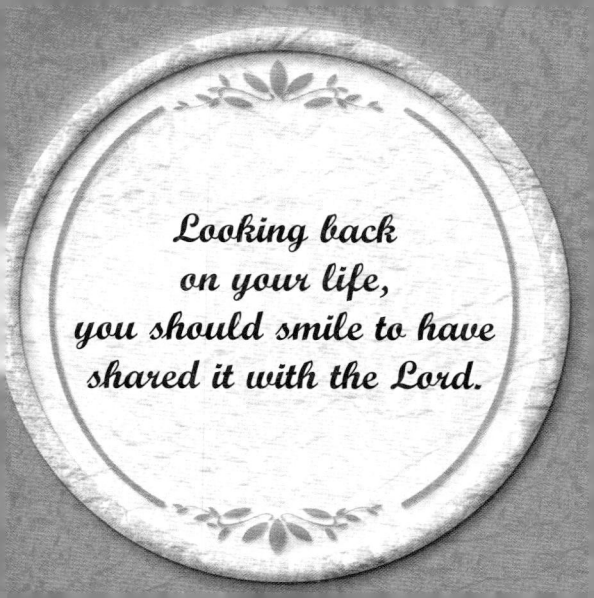

*Looking back
on your life,
you should smile to have
shared it with the Lord.*

Like a mother cares for her children, so does the Lord care for His. He keeps them warm when night turns cold and gives them everlasting love.

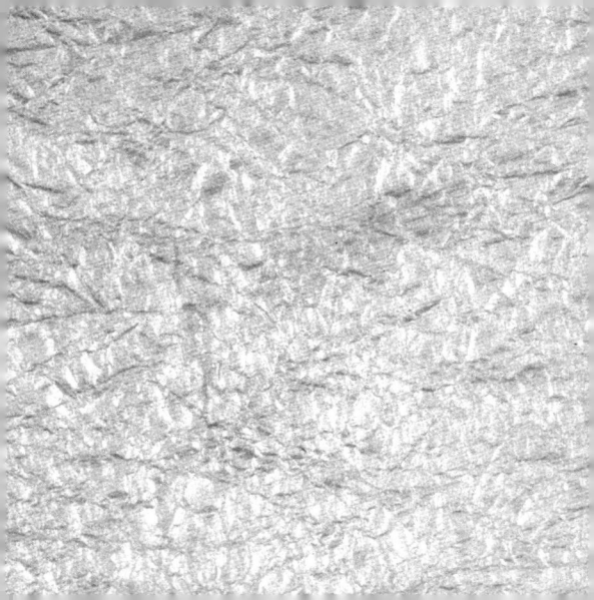